Stories
to
Treasure

CONTENTS

The Elves and the Shoemaker

The Elves and the Shoemaker

Once upon a time there was a shoemaker who, through no fault of his own, had become so poor that he had only enough leather left for one more pair of shoes.

"I must make these shoes the best ones I have ever made," he said to himself, "for they could be the last I ever make."

So he carefully cut the leather out and left the pieces ready to sew the next day when it was daylight. Then he blew out the candle and crept into bed.

Next morning he went to begin work and could hardly believe what he saw.

There on his workbench was the pair of shoes already made. He picked them up and looked at them.

"Well," he said, "not a stitch out of place. These shoes have been made by a master craftsman."

He put them in his window and that very day a customer came in to buy them.

"These shoes are the finest I have ever seen," cried the man and paid more than the usual price.

With the money, the shoemaker was able to buy enough leather to make two pairs of shoes and that night he cut it out and left it ready to sew the next day.

Once again, he found the shoes had already been sewn. Two beautiful pairs of shoes sat on the bench. Again he sold these for more than the usual price and had enough money to buy the leather for four pairs of shoes and these, too, he sold for a lot of money.

This went on for many days and soon the old shoemaker was making a comfortable living and no longer feared the future.

One day, just before Christmas, he said to his wife,

"Let's stay up late tonight, hide in the workshop and see if we can find out who has been helping us."

That night the two of them hid behind a cupboard in a corner of the workshop and waited to see if anything would happen. As the church clock struck midnight two tiny, barefoot elves in ragged clothes ran into the room. They climbed on the workbench and began stitching and sewing, as quickly as could be, all the leather that the shoemaker had left there.

The shoemaker and his wife watched in disbelief as the two tiny elves used up all the leather, neatly put the shoes they had made in pairs on the bench and then disappeared as quickly as they had come.

The old couple went to bed and next day the shoemaker's wife said to her husband,

"Those two elves have made us rich and I think we should show them how grateful we are."

He agreed and asked what they should do.

"Well," said his wife, "their clothes were ragged and they had no shoes on their feet so I think they must be very cold this winter. I will make them each little shirts, trousers and jackets and knit them long woollen socks and you can make them each a pair of shoes."

So that is what they did.

The shoemaker and his wife worked hard making the two suits and the two pairs of shoes for the elves. She knitted long, warm woollen stockings when she had finished the suits and then said to her husband,

"I think I have enough material to make hats for them too. Go to the chicken run and get me two long feathers to put in the hatbands. That will look very smart."

On Christmas Eve everything was finished and the shoemaker's wife wrapped all the clothes up into two little parcels and the shoemaker put them on the workbench instead of the pile of pieces of leather.

Again they hid and waited to see what would happen.

As midnight struck the two tiny elves appeared and scampered to the workbench and stopped in surprise at seeing the two parcels.

Chuckling, they opened them and burst into delighted laughter. They threw off their tattered clothes and dressed in the fine, new ones. Then they danced across the bench singing,

"Now we are so fine to see,
We will no longer work, not we."

Dancing and singing they ran across the floor and out of the door and were never seen again.

Nevertheless, the shoemaker continued to prosper and he and his wife lived happily ever after.

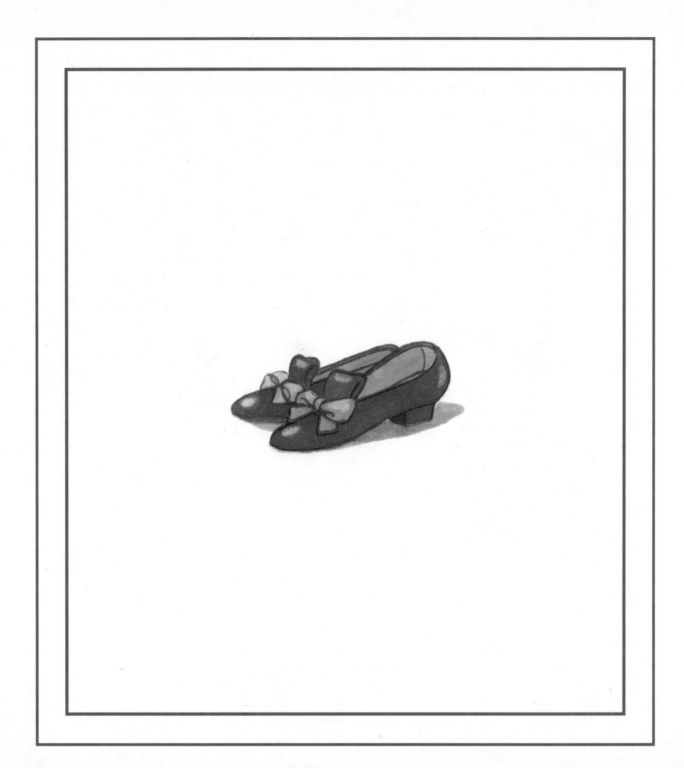

Sleeping Beauty

Sleeping Beauty

Once upon a time, in a far-off land, there lived a King and Queen who longed for a baby. Many years passed before their wish came true and a baby girl was born. The King and Queen were very happy and so they gave a huge banquet. They invited all their friends and there was much rejoicing in the palace.

The fairies of the kingdom had also been invited and after the banquet all the good fairies went to the little Princess's nursery. One by one they wished that she would grow up to be beautiful, clever and good.

The good fairies were busy making their wishes when, suddenly, the door opened and in walked the bad fairy.

"Why have I been left out?" she cried. "Why wasn't I invited to the banquet?"

Somehow, the King and Queen had forgotten to invite her.

Leaning over the baby's crib the bad fairy said,

"When you reach your fifteenth birthday you will be pricked by the spindle of a spinning wheel and will die."

With that she disappeared in a puff of smoke.

The last fairy had not yet bestowed her gift so she wished that the Princess would not die but only sleep for one hundred years.

The King ordered that all the spinning wheels in the country were to be destroyed.

The years passed and the little Princess grew into a beautiful, young girl. The bad fairy's curse was forgotten and everyone in the palace was happy.

On her fifteenth birthday the Princess was exploring the palace and opened a door at the top of an old staircase. Inside the room she saw an old woman turning a strange wheel.

"What are you doing?" asked the Princess who, of course, had never seen a spinning wheel before.

"I am spinning," said the old woman. "Would you like to try?"

As soon as the Princess picked up the spindle she pricked her finger and fell to the floor in a deep sleep.

When the King and Queen found her they laid her down on her bed. The good fairies came and said that the Princess would only wake up when a Prince kissed her and, so that she would not be on her own during her long sleep, they waved their wands and everyone and everything in the palace fell asleep.

King, Queen, soldiers, courtiers and servants, horses, dogs, mice and rats, all slept and while they slept a magic forest grew round the palace to protect it.

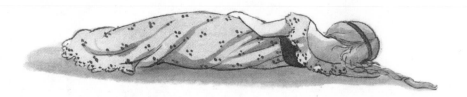

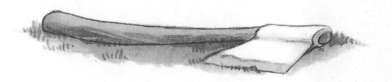

Years passed and, as legends about the beautiful, sleeping Princess grew, many young men tried to reach the palace but all failed to pierce the magic forest.

Exactly one hundred years later, to the day, a young Prince was hunting near the palace and asked a woodcutter about it.

"My old grandfather told me a curse was put on the Princess and that she is inside, fast asleep, with all the people in the palace, and that she can only be awoken by the kiss of a Prince. No-one has ever managed to get through that forest, though," added the woodcutter.

The Prince listened in growing excitement to the story and decided he would be the Prince who would awaken the sleeping Princess. He thanked the woodcutter and made his way towards the forest round the palace.

As he approached he took out his sword but was astounded to find the branches parting

before him and that he had no need to struggle.

As the palace gates came into view he could see the sleeping guards. He pushed the gates open and went in. The whole palace was asleep, even the dogs in the kennels.

The brave, young Prince made his way through dusty rooms searching for the sleeping Princess.

At last he found her lying on her bed. She looked so beautiful and peaceful as she lay there.

He knelt down and very gently kissed her on the lips. Her eyes opened and she awoke.

Soon all the palace was rousing from its long sleep. Courtiers, soldiers, cooks and stablemen – all awoke and stretched and wondered what was happening. The King and Queen hurried to see their daughter and found her wide awake at last.

The Prince and the Princess fell in love and the King and Queen happily agreed to the marriage and they all lived happily ever after.

Puss in Boots

Puss in Boots

Once upon a time there was a poor miller who had three sons who, when he died, left only his mill, his donkey and his cat. The eldest son took the mill, the second the donkey and the youngest was left with nothing but the cat.

"My brothers have done well," said the youngest son. "They can make a living with the mill and the donkey together but how can I manage?"

"Don't be sad, master," said the cat. "Just give me a sack and a pair of boots and you will soon see that you have the best bargain."

The miller's son was astonished to hear the cat talk.

"A talking cat might just be clever enough to do anything," he thought, so he bought a pair of leather boots for the cat and said, "Well now, Puss in Boots, what are you going to do?"

"Wait and see!" said the cat and, swinging a sack over his shoulder, he set out into the woods.

He hid by a rabbit warren and soon tricked a silly young rabbit into his sack. Then off he went to the King's palace and demanded to see the King.

"Your Majesty," he said, "I have brought a gift from my master, the Marquis of Carabas." This was the title he had invented for the miller's son.

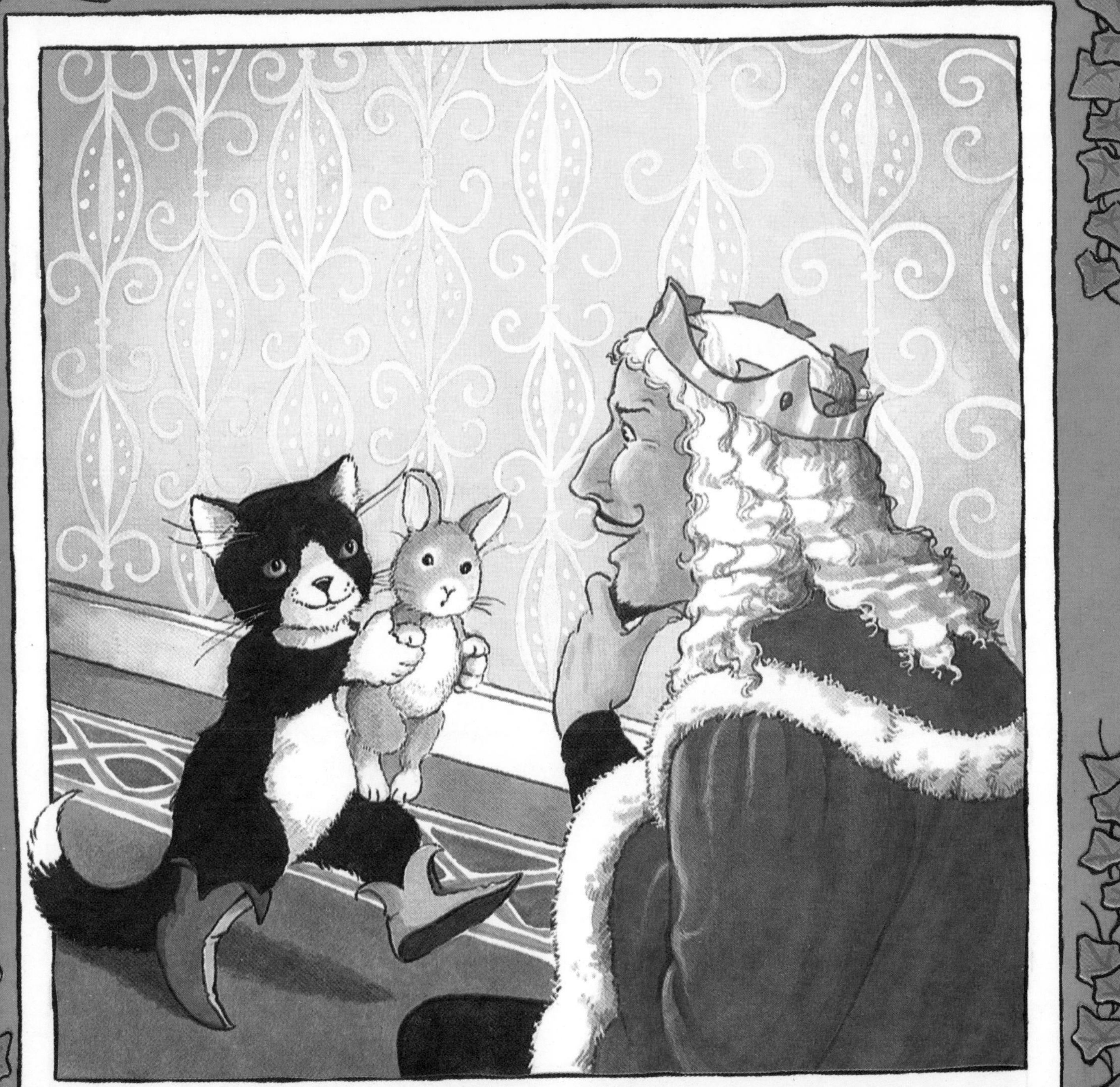

As the King was pleased with the rabbit, Puss brought him more gifts, each time saying they were from his master.

One day the cat heard that the King and his beautiful daughter were to drive by the river so he went to his master and said,

"Do just as I say and you will be rich. Go and bathe in the river."

He did as he was bid and the cat hid his clothes. As the royal coach came by the cat shouted,

"Help! My master, the Marquis of Carabas is drowning."

The King, recognising Puss, ordered his guards to save the young man.

"Thank you, Your Majesty," said Puss, "but what can my master do? His clothes have been stolen."

The King immediately sent for a suit of clothes and then invited the miller's son to ride with him. He looked so handsome in his new clothes that the beautiful Princess fell in love with him.

Meanwhile the cat hurried ahead, first to a field where some men were working and then to where a shepherd was with his sheep. He shouted to them all,

"The King is coming. Tell him the fields and the sheep belong to the Marquis of Carabas or you'll be in trouble."

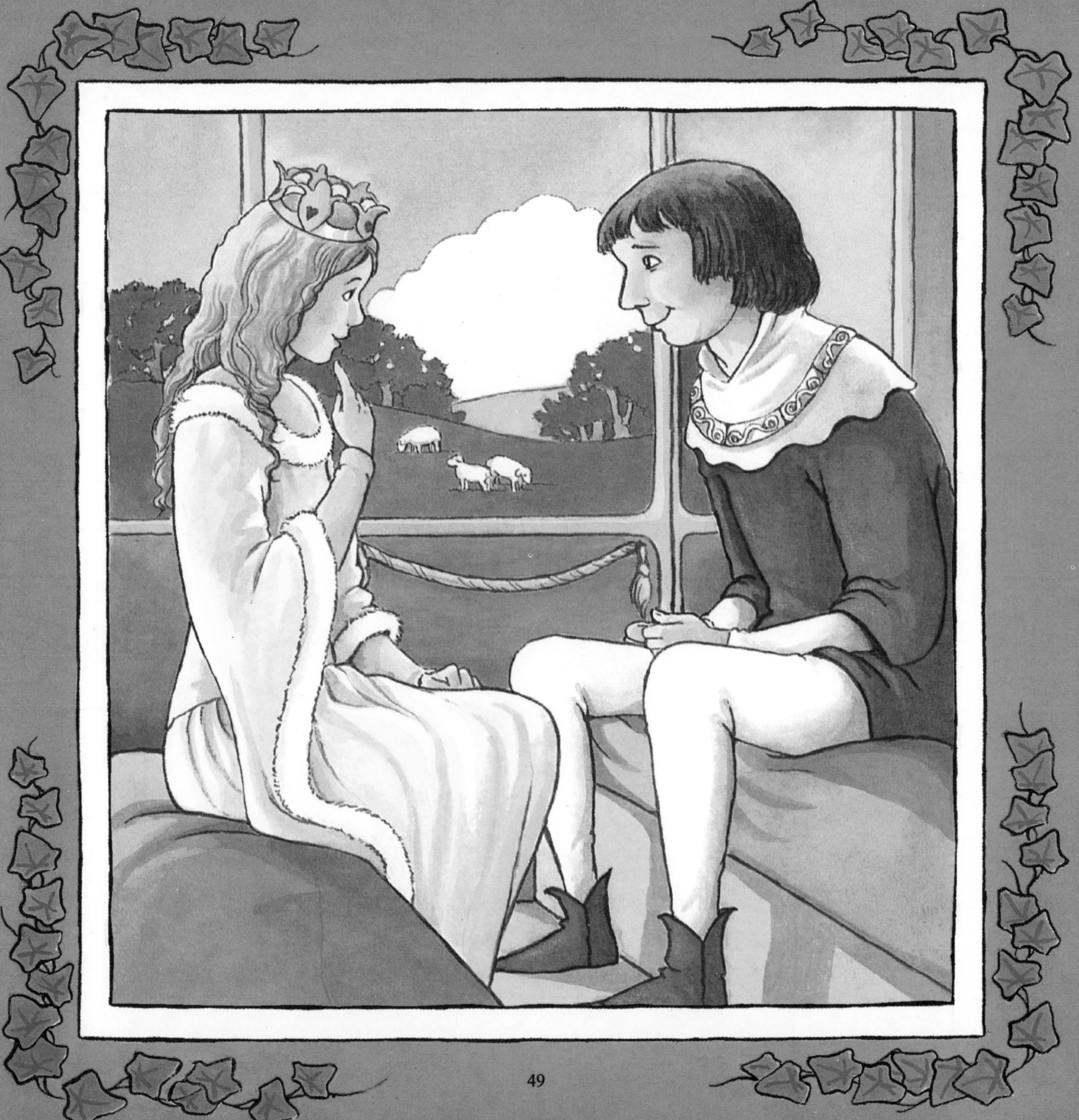

He looked so fierce that they did as he said.

Now the fields really belonged to an ogre who lived in a nearby castle. Puss knew of this ogre and called at the castle door.

"Sir," said Puss to the ogre, "I have been told you are able to turn yourself into an elephant or a lion."

"Indeed I can," said the ogre proudly and the next moment there stood a great lion which roared mightily.

Puss was so frightened that he jumped straight up to the top of a tall cupboard.

When the ogre changed himself back Puss jumped down.

"Well," said the cunning cat, "that was very fine but I have also heard it said that you can change yourself into something very small and I am sure that is impossible."

"Impossible?" growled the ogre, deeply insulted. "Nothing is impossible for me!"

In the twinkling of an eye there appeared a tiny fieldmouse scampering across the floor. With one leap the clever cat caught the mouse and gobbled him up and that was the end of the fierce ogre.

Meanwhile, the King, with his daughter and the miller's son, had seen the castle and decided to call on its owner.

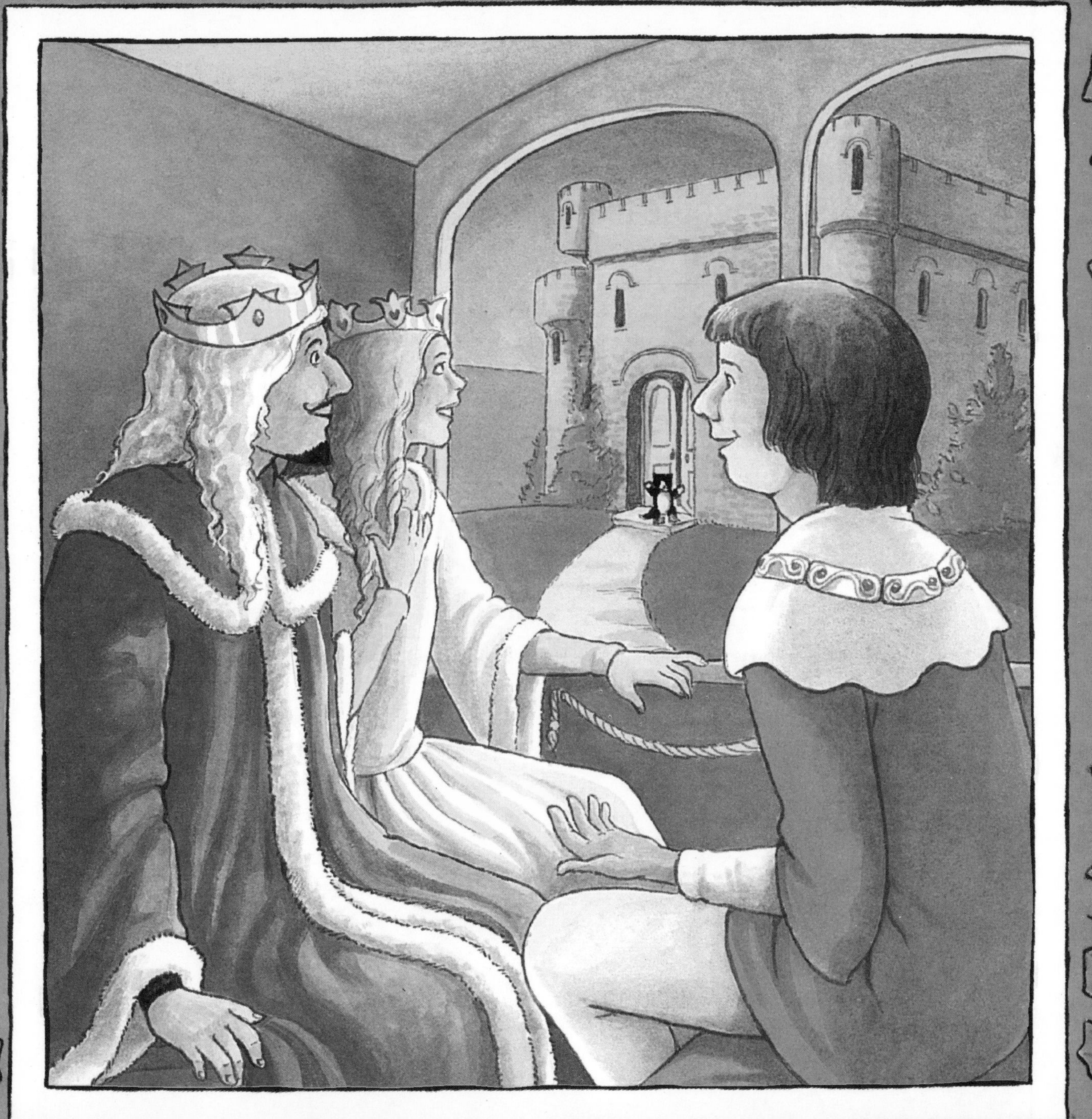

The coach rolled up to the castle door and there was Puss in Boots.

"Welcome to the castle of my master, the Marquis of Carabas!" he called, winking at the miller's son.

The King was delighted to see his new young friend lived in such a splendid castle and was pleased to be invited to the feast that had been prepared.

After the feast, the King declared that, since the Marquis and the Princess were obviously in love, they ought to get married. So they did and lived happily ever after.

As for Puss in Boots he lived off the fat of the land with his master until the end of his days!

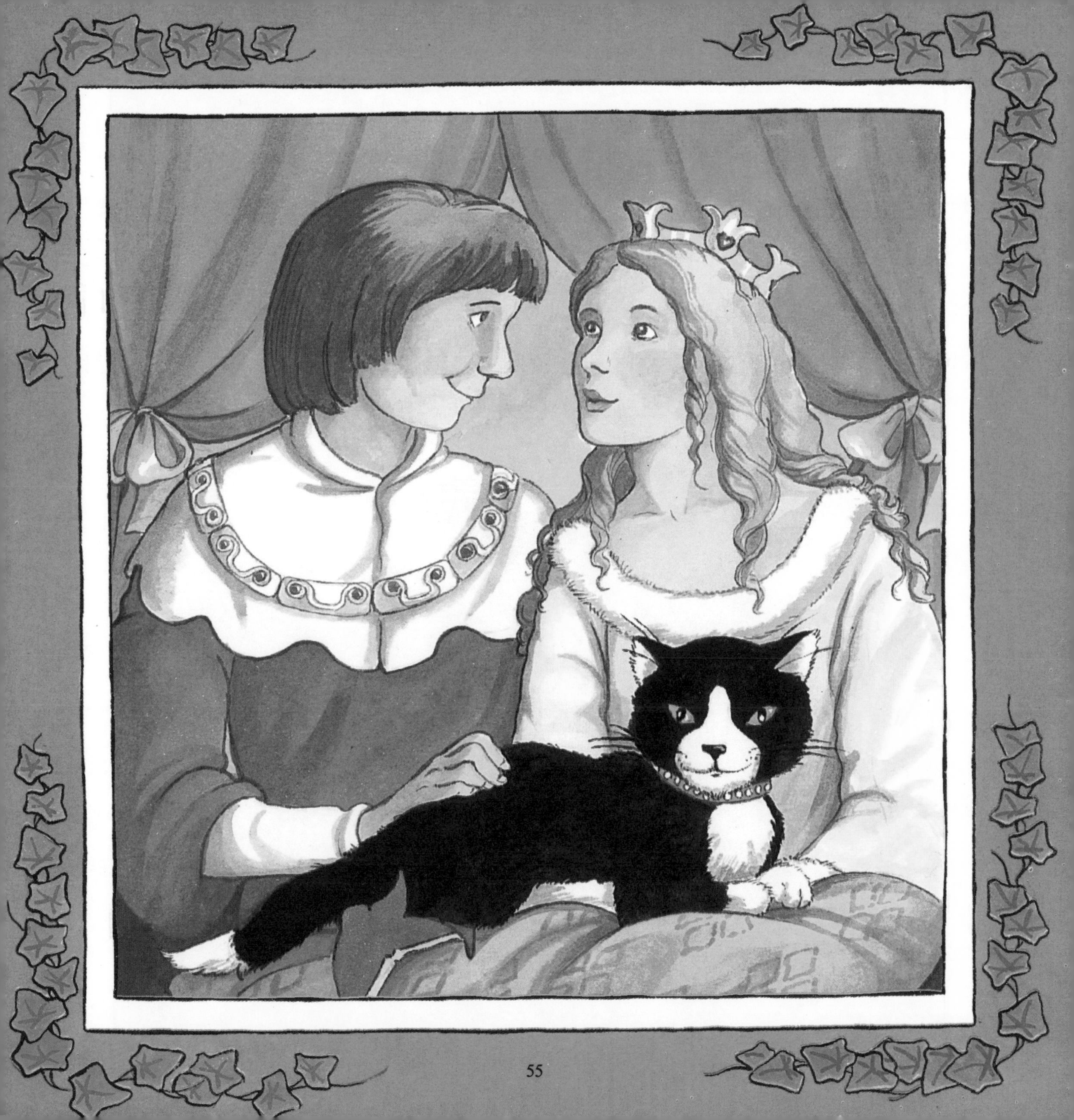

Thumbelina

Thumbelina

Once upon a time there was a woman who longed for a child. So desperate was she that she asked for help from a witch who gave her a seed and told her to watch what happened when she planted it in a flowerpot.

The plant grew and flowered and, when the bud opened, there, inside, was a tiny girl, no bigger than your thumb. The woman loved her dearly and called her Thumbelina.

Thumbelina's bed was a walnut shell with a rose-petal coverlet. She could row the walnut shell across a bowl of water using a pair of horsehairs as oars.

One night while Thumbelina was asleep in her walnut shell a hideous toad came clambering through the open window.

"What a pretty young girl. She would make a lovely bride for my son," the toad croaked to himself and, picking up the walnut shell with the sleeping Thumbelina inside, he hopped away.

When Thumbelina awoke she found herself on the leaf of a waterlily floating in the middle of a pond and the toad told her she was to marry his son.

She was horrified and burst into tears but the toads were pleased because toads cry only when they are happy.

A butterfly heard her sobs and used one of the horsehairs to tow the leaf to the bank while the toads were away. Thumbelina thanked her but before she could climb on to the bank a large stag beetle flew down, picked her up and carried her high into a tree. He thought she was beautiful and gave her a sweet flower to eat and paid her compliments.

However, when the other beetles came to see the new arrival they said she was ugly.

"Fancy," said one, "she has only two legs. How strange!"

"And no feelers at all!" added another. "She's very peculiar!"

In truth, Thumbelina was very beautiful but the stag beetle began to believe she was not and, deciding to let her go, he carried her to the ground and left her on a daisy.

As it was summer, Thumbelina could find food for herself and keep warm but when winter came she was very unhappy for the snow covered all her food and her clothes were too worn and ragged to be of any use.

She was sitting shivering one day when a fieldmouse found her and, taking pity on her, invited her into her warm, little house and took care of her.

Thumbelina was grateful to the little fieldmouse for saving her and spent many hours telling her stories. The old, blind mole used to listen too and, before long, he had fallen in love with her. He dug her a tunnel so that she could walk safely and one day Thumbelina found a swallow just inside the entrance. The mole thought he was dead but Thumbelina nursed him until he could fly away.

Soon the mole asked her to marry him and the fieldmouse told her how lucky she was. Thumbelina, however, did not want to live underground and never see the sun or the flowers again.

The mouse helped Thumbelina spin her trousseau and, just before the wedding, Thumbelina went.into the sunshine for the last time and asked the flowers to give the swallow her love if ever they saw him again.

Just then there came a joyous 'tweet' and the swallow was diving and swooping above her.

"Come with me! Come with me! I'll take you to my warm, summer lands and you can live there and be happy," sang the swallow.

So Thumbelina thanked the kind, little fieldmouse and asked her to explain to the old, blind mole that she could not live under the ground.

Then Thumbelina said goodbye to the flowers and climbed on the swallow's back. Up he flew, higher and higher, carrying her over fields and forests and then the deep blue of the sea. The air grew warmer as the swallow spiralled down towards some ruins; great tumbled pieces of stone with broken columns covered in greenery.

Thumbelina climbed down and looked round. From the flower trumpets jumped little people her own size.

"I am the Prince of the Flower Spirits," said one. "Welcome to our land."

Soon the Prince and Thumbelina fell in love and were married and lived happily ever after.

Pinocchio

Pinocchio

Once upon a time there was an old wood-carver called Geppetto. He was lonely and longed for a son so he decided to make himself a puppet for company. The Blue Fairy heard his wish and, when he had finished the carving, she made the puppet come to life. Geppetto was overjoyed and decided to call his new son Pinocchio.

However, Pinocchio was naughty, kicked his new father's shins and ran out into the street into the arms of a policeman. Poor Geppetto, for the policeman believed that he had beaten Pinocchio and took him to prison. So Pinocchio went back to the house where now he could do just as he liked.

After he had eaten he sat by the fire and a tiny cricket warned him,

"Beware! Boys who don't listen to their fathers are always sorry later." Naughty Pinocchio ignored this advice.

When Geppetto came back he found Pinocchio asleep so close to the fire that his wooden feet had burned away. Geppetto made some more and told him he must go to school like a real boy but he was so poor he had to sell his coat to buy Pinocchio a spelling book and some clothes.

Pinocchio was sorry and said he would be a good boy at school but, on the way there, he heard some music and went to see what was happening.

The music was from a travelling puppet show and Pinocchio was thrilled to see puppets, just like himself, on the stage and hurried to join them. It was a disaster, for the other puppets had long strings and he soon became entangled.

The puppet master was furious and threatened to throw him on the fire as fuel but when Pinocchio begged for his life the puppet master relented.

"I'll throw Harlequin on instead."

"No! No!" cried Pinocchio. "It's not his fault. Burn me after all."

He was touched by Pinocchio's bravery and gave him some gold coins as a reward to take home to Geppetto.

Someone saw Pinocchio's money!

Going home to give the money to Geppetto he met the thieving cat and fox who had seen him get the money but clever Pinocchio hid it from the wicked pair in his shoe. They were angry and left him tied to the branch of a tree.

Now, the Blue Fairy had been watching over Pinocchio all this time and she rescued him and asked him about the money. He lied and said he had lost it. As he lied his nose grew longer and longer. The Blue Fairy laughed and said,

"That's what will always happen when you tell lies, Pinocchio!"

"I'm sorry! I'll be good!" he cried.

So she called some woodpeckers to peck his nose back to its right size.

Pinocchio promised to tell the truth and set off again for home. He really did mean to be good but, alas, he met a naughty boy who told him about a place called Toyland.

"There's no school, no rules to keep and lollipops grow on trees there!"

Pinocchio had a wonderful time at first but having fun all day and not doing any work was very bad for him, and all the other boys, and, bit by bit, they found they were all turning into donkeys with furry ears. Pinocchio was sold to a circus and made to do tricks. When he fell and hurt his leg and could no longer work, the cruel ringmaster threw him over a cliff into the sea.

As soon as Pinocchio fell into the water the magic spell from Toyland was broken and he was once more a puppet.

While he was floating in the sea he thought how sorry he was for all his naughty deeds and he was afraid that he would never see Geppetto again.

Suddenly he was swallowed by a huge fish. Poor Pinocchio was terrified for he could see nothing in the darkness. When he could stand he saw a tiny light and walked towards it.

Wonder of wonders! It was a little fire built by Geppetto who had been swallowed by the very same fish when he had been sailing and searching for his lost Pinocchio.

Joyfully they hugged each other and then Geppetto said tearfully,

"Oh, Pinocchio, now we are both marooned in this terrible place."

"Don't worry, Father. We'll think of something," said Pinocchio bravely. "I know! Let's build the fire bigger and see what happens."

So they did until all the smoke made the fish sneeze and, with his third sneeze, out they shot on to a beach and there was the Blue Fairy, waiting for them.

"Pinocchio, this is your reward for saving Geppetto's life."

Pinocchio became a real boy and he and Geppetto lived happily ever after.

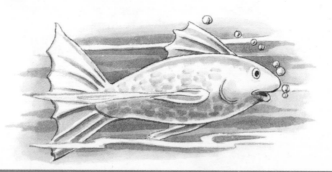

Rapunzel

Rapunzel

Once upon a time a husband and wife lived happily in a house whose upstairs window overlooked a beautiful garden. In this garden everything grew in profusion. The trees were laden with fruit and the flowers were brightly coloured. One day as the wife hung out her washing she noticed how well the rapunzel herb had grown. From then on each day she would sit at the window longing for a taste.

However, as a horrid witch lived next door, whom everyone feared, she knew that she would not be able to have any and began to pine away and grow weak and ill.

Her husband, fearing for her life, decided to take matters into his own hands. He climbed over the high wall and filled his basket with the rapunzel herb. The witch caught him in the act.

"How dare you come into my garden and steal my herbs!" she cried angrily.

The terrified man told the witch about his wife's craving and how he hoped the rapunzel would cure her and the witch eventually allowed him to take the herb on the condition that they would give her their first-born child. The man nodded his head in agreement and rushed back to his wife.

The herb did make her well and not long afterwards she had a baby girl. The witch came and took the baby away and named her Rapunzel after the herb.

The years passed and the couple could only watch their child from the upstairs window as she played happily in the witch's garden.

She was such a pretty little girl with long, golden hair.

When Rapunzel was twelve years old the witch decided to lock her in a high tower so she could not run away. When Rapunzel was in the topmost room the witch put a spell on the staircase and door so Rapunzel could not find them.

Rapunzel's hair was in a long plait. Each day, when the witch visited her, she would call out,

"Rapunzel, Rapunzel,
Let down your long hair!"

Rapunzel would let her long plait fall down the tower and the witch would climb up it.

One day a passing Prince heard the witch calling out and could not believe it when he saw the plait come down and the witch climb up it. As he was full of curiosity he waited until the witch had left and then he called out,

"Rapunzel, Rapunzel,
Let down your long hair!"

When the plait came down the Prince climbed up it and was amazed to see the beautiful girl. Gently, he began talking to her and soon Rapunzel and he became friends. The Prince visited her often after that as he loved to hear her sing.

One day, however, Rapunzel asked the witch,

"Why is it that the Prince climbs up my hair so much faster than you do?"

The witch was very angry at being deceived and the next day, when she visited Rapunzel, she cut off her hair and led her deep into the forest where she abandoned her.

The witch returned to the tower and, when the Prince called out, she tied the plait to the window and let it down. What a shock the Prince got when he saw the witch.

"You will never see Rapunzel again," she screeched as she pulled his hands from the hair.

The Prince fell headlong into a clump of thorny bushes. They broke his fall but their thorns scratched his eyes so that he could not see. His horse had fled at the sound of the witch's voice and the Prince stumbled around the forest for many days, surviving on berries and water from streams.

Over the weeks the Prince had gradually become accustomed to the sounds of the forest as he wandered blind and lonely through the countryside but, one day, he heard a new sound he thought he recognised. Rapunzel was singing. He stumbled towards the sound calling her name.

Suddenly Rapunzel saw him and ran into his arms. As she kissed him his eyes were healed and he could see her.

The Prince took Rapunzel to meet his father and when he heard the story he banished the witch from the kingdom.

Rapunzel was reunited with her parents and later she and the Prince were married.

The Steadfast Tin Soldier

The Steadfast Tin Soldier

Once upon a time there was a little boy named Peter who lived in a nice house with his mother and father and his nanny. He was a very lucky little boy as he had lots of toys and a nursery to play in. On Peter's birthday he was given a box of twenty-five tin soldiers as a present. One little tin soldier had only one leg but that did not seem to matter as he could still stand perfectly to attention.

That night when Peter went to bed he forgot to put the little tin soldier back into the box with his twenty-four comrades and left him on a shelf in the nursery.

From there he could see a beautiful ballerina who was balanced on one leg in front of a toy castle with a lake.

The little tin soldier thought that she was the prettiest thing he had ever seen and he fell in love with her.

There were lots of other toys in the nursery and at midnight they all came to life and were able to talk and play as they wished.

The little tin soldier, however, was far too shy to speak to the ballerina. He just stared at her and hoped that she would notice him. After a while the ballerina jumped down to the floor, so the little tin soldier bravely did the same. But he still could not pluck up enough courage to speak to her so he joined Teddy for a game of cricket. The ballerina watched them play but she, too, was shy and could not bring herself to speak to them or to join in the fun. By daybreak the toys had all returned to their boxes or place on the shelves as they could not let Peter see them playing. He did not know that they came to life at midnight.

The tin soldier had missed his chance of speaking to the ballerina. Maybe the next night he would find some extra courage to enable him to speak to her.

The next morning, before going to school, Peter played with his toys and as it was such a nice day, he opened the window and stood the tin soldiers to attention on the window-sill. Just before he left, Peter packed the tin soldiers away but he forgot the one-legged one.

The little tin soldier stood proudly to attention on the window-sill until, suddenly, a great gust of wind blew the curtains and knocked him out of the window.

He landed on the pavement with a thud.

It began to rain. First one drop fell and then another and soon it was pouring down.

The poor tin soldier was getting wetter and wetter. How he wished that he was in the nursery with the little ballerina and the rest of the toys. He wondered whether any of them had missed him.

"Maybe I will be left here all day," thought the little soldier, sadly.

As luck would have it, two small boys came out to play in the rain. As they were splashing about in the puddles they were surprised to find the little tin soldier on the pavement.

"Look!" said one of them. "This little soldier has only got one leg."

"I think we should make a boat for him," said the other one. "Then he can sail down the road and it won't matter that he only has one leg." The boys looked around and found a newspaper. "This will do," said one. "We can make a boat out of this."

So that is what they did. They folded and shaped the paper until it looked like a really good boat. They put the tin soldier in this and it sailed along the gutter. The water was flowing quite quickly and the poor little tin soldier wondered where he was going. He tried very hard to be brave and stared straight ahead as he sailed away from the two boys.

The boat, with the little tin soldier sitting in it, rushed along the gutter and into a drain. It was very dark in the drain and, although he tried not to be, the little tin soldier was rather frightened. The walls of the drain were dirty and there were several rats swimming about in the water.

How the little tin soldier longed to be back in the nursery with the other toys. He tried to keep up his spirits by thinking about the pretty ballerina. He wondered whether she had noticed that he was not in his usual place in the nursery.

As all these thoughts were going through the little tin soldier's head, the paper boat was rushing along the drain towards the river.

Finally, the paper boat was washed into the river and it fell apart. The poor little tin soldier fell into the water and began to sink to the river bed.

By this time he was really frightened and thought that his last moment had come. He was very sad to think that he would never see the ballerina again.

The weed waved in his face as he sank to the rocks on the river bed. Suddenly, there was a swirl in the water and the face of a big fish appeared in front of the little tin soldier. What a fright he got! Then suddenly everything went dark. The greedy fish had swallowed the little tin soldier and he was now inside the fish. No wonder it was dark and he could not see where he was. But help was at hand. The fish began to shake and twist and then was still. A fisherman had caught the fish with his rod. As it was such a nice, big fish he decided to sell it to a fishmonger. And that is what he did. As luck would have it, the person who bought the fish was none other than the cook from the house where the little tin soldier used to live.

The cook took the fish home, put it on the kitchen table and began to prepare it for dinner. As she cut into it, light burst in on the little tin soldier. He blinked and looked around in amazement. He recognised the cook and his surroundings immediately. He could not believe his luck in arriving back in the kitchen of the house where he used to live.

The cook was as surprised as the little tin soldier. She, of course, recognised the one-legged soldier as the one from Peter's nursery.

"However did you get in there?" she asked as she stared down at the tin soldier emerging from inside the fish. What a nice surprise Peter was going to get when he came home. He had been very upset when the little tin soldier was lost and had looked everywhere for him. The tin soldier was happy because he would see the ballerina again. "Maybe I will speak to her tonight," he thought, as the cook carried him upstairs to the nursery.

There was a lovely, roaring fire in the nursery when the cook took the tin soldier back there.

"I think I will put you on the mantelpiece for now," she said to him. "Then Peter will see you as soon as he comes in."

To the tin soldier's amazement the ballerina was also on the mantelpiece. It seemed to the tin soldier that she had been waiting for him. They gazed at each other but were still too shy to speak.

The cook had not noticed that the window in the nursery was left open. The wind began to blow and was soon causing quite a draught. Suddenly, an extra strong gust blew the ballerina and the tin soldier off the mantelpiece and into the fire. At that moment Peter came into the nursery and saw his toys fall.

"I must rescue them," he cried and he quickly grabbed the poker and raked them out of the fire and on to the hearth.

Peter left the toys on the hearth for quite a long time as he knew that they would be hot from the flames. As he waited for them to cool down he wondered where his one-legged soldier had been and how he had got on to the mantelpiece. He had no idea of the adventure that the little tin soldier had had.

When he finally picked up the toys from the hearth, Peter found that their two bases had melted together into the shape of a heart. So the tin soldier and his beloved ballerina were joined together and were never separated again.

To this day they marvel how it was that the cook bought the very fish which had swallowed the tin soldier and they are very pleased that she did.

Goldilocks and the Three Bears

Goldilocks and the Three Bears

Once upon a time there was a little girl called Goldilocks. She had been given that name because her hair shone like gold in the sun.

Her mother had warned her not to wander into the great forest which lay close to their cottage, for fear she would get lost, but Goldilocks did not always do as she was told and, one day when she was bored with all her toys, she made sure her mother was not watching and ran quickly down the path into the great forest, certain that she would be able to find her way home.

She wandered happily in the forest looking at all the birds and flowers and once she saw some rabbits playing. When she was tired she decided to go home but, on turning round, she found the paths looked very different and could not find the right one. She soon realised she was lost and did not even know in which direction her home lay.

"Oh, I wish I had listened to Mother," she said as she sank down on a log and burst into tears.

Bravely, she dried her tears and, when she had walked a little further, saw a tiny cottage among the trees.

Goldilocks crept towards the cottage, knocked on the door and peeped in the windows but no-one came. She pushed the front door and it opened.

"What a pretty cottage," thought Goldilocks and saw that there were three bowls of porridge on the table – a big one, a middle-sized one and a small one.

She was hungry by this time and tried the big bowl but that was too hot. She tried the middle-sized bowl but that was too cold. She tried the small bowl and that was just right and before she knew what she had done she had eaten it all up.

By the fire were three chairs – a big one, a middle-sized one and small one. Goldilocks tried the big chair but that was too high. She tried the middle-sized one but that was too hard. When she tried the small one that was just right but it broke as she sat down.

Then she saw the staircase. Upstairs were three beds – a big one, a middle-sized one and a small one. Goldilocks tried the big bed but that was too hard. She tried the middle-sized one but that was too soft. The small one was just right and soon she was fast asleep.

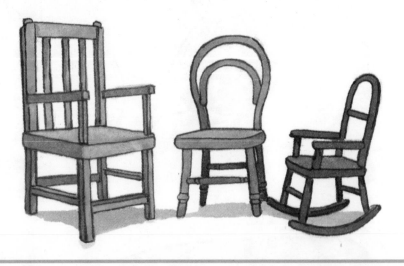

The cottage belonged to three bears and when they returned Father Bear growled in his big, loud voice,

"Who has been tasting my porridge?"

"Who has been tasting my porridge?" said Mother Bear in her soft, gentle voice.

"Who has eaten all my porridge up and left me none at all?" cried Baby Bear in his squeaky, little voice.

Then Father Bear saw his chair and growled in his big, loud voice,

"Who has been sitting in my chair?"

"Who has been sitting in my chair?" said Mother Bear in her soft, gentle voice.

"And who has been sitting in my chair and broken it all to pieces?" cried Baby Bear in his squeaky, little voice.

Father Bear said in his big, loud voice,

"Look, there are muddy footprints on the floor leading upstairs."

So the three bears followed the footprints up the stairs.

"Who has been sleeping in my bed?" growled Father Bear in his big, loud voice.

"Who has been sleeping in my bed?" said Mother Bear in her soft, gentle voice.

"Who has been sleeping in my bed and is still there, fast asleep?" cried Baby Bear in his squeaky, little voice.

Astonished, the three bears all looked at Baby Bear's bed where, fast asleep, lay Goldilocks with her golden hair spread across the pillow.

"She ate all my porridge and she broke my chair," wailed Baby Bear.

Goldilocks was dreaming and the voices from downstairs had become part of her dream but Baby Bear's squeaky, little voice in her ear woke her up and she sat up rubbing her eyes.

"Oh, my!" she screamed and, jumping out of bed, ran across the bedroom, down the stairs and out of the door before the bears could move.

She ran and ran, down the path, across the clearing and into the woods, until she came to her own little cottage.

Goldilocks never went wandering in the great forest again.

Snow White & The Seven Dwarves

Snow White & The Seven Dwarves

Once upon a time a queen sat sewing by her window. Snow flakes were falling outside and, as she watched them settling on her black, ebony windowsill, she pricked her finger and a drop of red blood fell on to the snow. Then she thought, "I wish I had a daughter with skin as white as snow, with cheeks as red as blood and hair as black as ebony."

The queen's wish came true and she gave birth to a beautiful baby girl whom she named Snow White and her skin was as white as snow, her cheeks as red as blood and her hair as black as ebony. Sadly, the queen died soon after Snow White was born but the king loved his daughter and spent hours playing with her. She grew up to be sweet-natured and was loved by everyone.

The king, however, was lonely and he married again so Snow White now had a stepmother but she was not as loving and kind as Snow White's own mother.

The new queen was very beautiful but she was also evil and vain and could not bear to think that anyone might be lovelier than she. She had a magic mirror which she would look into every day and ask,

"Mirror, mirror on the wall,
Who is the fairest of them all?"

The mirror's answer was always the same, "Thou art the fairest."

The queen was happy with the answer and all was well. However, as the years passed, Snow White grew into a beautiful young woman and one fateful day, the queen asked her mirror the usual question,

"Mirror, mirror on the wall,
Who is the fairest of them all?"

The mirror answered,

"Thou art fair and beauteous to see,
But Snow White is fairer far than thee."

At these words the queen flew into a rage. She wanted to be the fairest in the land.

She was so angry that she sent for her huntsman and ordered him to take Snow White into the forest and kill her. The huntsman took Snow White but, when they were deep in the forest, he told her to run away. He was very fond of her and could not bring himself to kill her. He killed a deer and took its heart back to the wicked queen to convince her that Snow White was actually dead.

Snow White wandered through the woods and soon she began to feel hungry and frightened. She looked for berries to eat and somewhere to sleep.

Suddenly she saw a tiny cottage. She went up to the door and knocked. There was no answer so she went inside. The room was cosy and warm and the table was laid for supper. A stew bubbled in the pot which hung over the fire and it smelt so good that Snow White helped herself to some. Then, feeling sleepy, she went upstairs.

There she found seven little beds. She was so tired that she decided to lie down until the owners of the cottage came home. The cottage belonged to seven dwarves who worked in the mountains digging for gold. When they came home they saw immediately that all was not right; there was a dirty plate on the table! They all crept up the stairs and then one of them whispered, "Look, someone is sleeping in my bed." His brothers were amazed.

"How lovely she is," they whispered and, taking care not to wake Snow White they decided to let her sleep and went downstairs.

When Snow White woke up, the dwarves surrounded her bed. She was a little afraid but they spoke kindly to her asking who she was and why she had come. When they had heard her story the dwarves took pity on Snow White and said that she was to stay with them where she would be safe.

They would look after her, and in return she would keep the cottage clean and cook their meals. Snow White soon settled into her new home and was very happy. The dwarves warned Snow White not to open the door to anyone while they were away.

But one day, back at the castle, the wicked queen looked into her magic mirror and asked,

"Mirror, mirror, on the wall,
Who is the fairest of them all?"

And the mirror replied,

"Queen, thou art of beauty rare,
But Snow White living in the glen,
With the seven little men,
Is a thousand times more fair."

When the queen realised that the huntsman had deceived her she was terribly angry. She locked herself in her secret room and brewed a horrible poison which she put into a rosy, red apple.

As she did not want Snow White to recognise her, she disguised herself as a peasant woman before setting off for the dwarves' home. When she arrived at the cottage she knocked on the door and begged to be let in. Snow White, however, had remembered the dwarves' warning not to open the door to strangers so she refused. "Silly girl," said the queen. "I've brought you a lovely apple. Please take it."

After the queen had gone, Snow White looked at the rosy, red apple. It was very tempting so she took a large bite. Immediately, she fell lifeless to the floor.

In the evening when the dwarves returned home from work as usual they could not believe their eyes when they found Snow White lying on the floor. They tried every way they could to revive her but it was no good. Sadly, they gave up and accepted the fact that she would never smile or speak to them again.

The seven dwarves made a beautiful, crystal coffin for Snow White, which they placed in a forest glade. They loved her so much they could not bear to bury her in the dark earth where they would never see her again. Every day they brought fresh flowers and placed them round the crystal coffin and wept for her.

Then, one day, a prince went riding in the forest and found the dwarves sitting around the coffin. When he saw Snow White lying there he fell in love with her and asked the dwarves who she was and what had happened to her. As they told him her story he opened the coffin and lifted Snow White into his arms. As he did so, the piece of apple, which the dwarves had not known was lodged in her throat, fell from her mouth. Immediately, she opened her eyes and on seeing the handsome prince she fell in love with him.

The prince asked Snow White to go with him to his father's palace. Snow White, of course, said yes, but she was sad to say goodbye to her seven little friends who had been so kind to her. They would also miss Snow White but they wanted her to be happy and they gave the couple their blessing. Back at the castle the evil queen could not believe it when her mirror said,

"Queen, although you are of beauty rare,
Snow White is a thousand times more fair."

She was so furious that she choked and died. Now Snow White had nothing to fear from the evil queen and she lived happily ever after with her prince in a beautiful palace, where they were often visited by the seven dwarves.

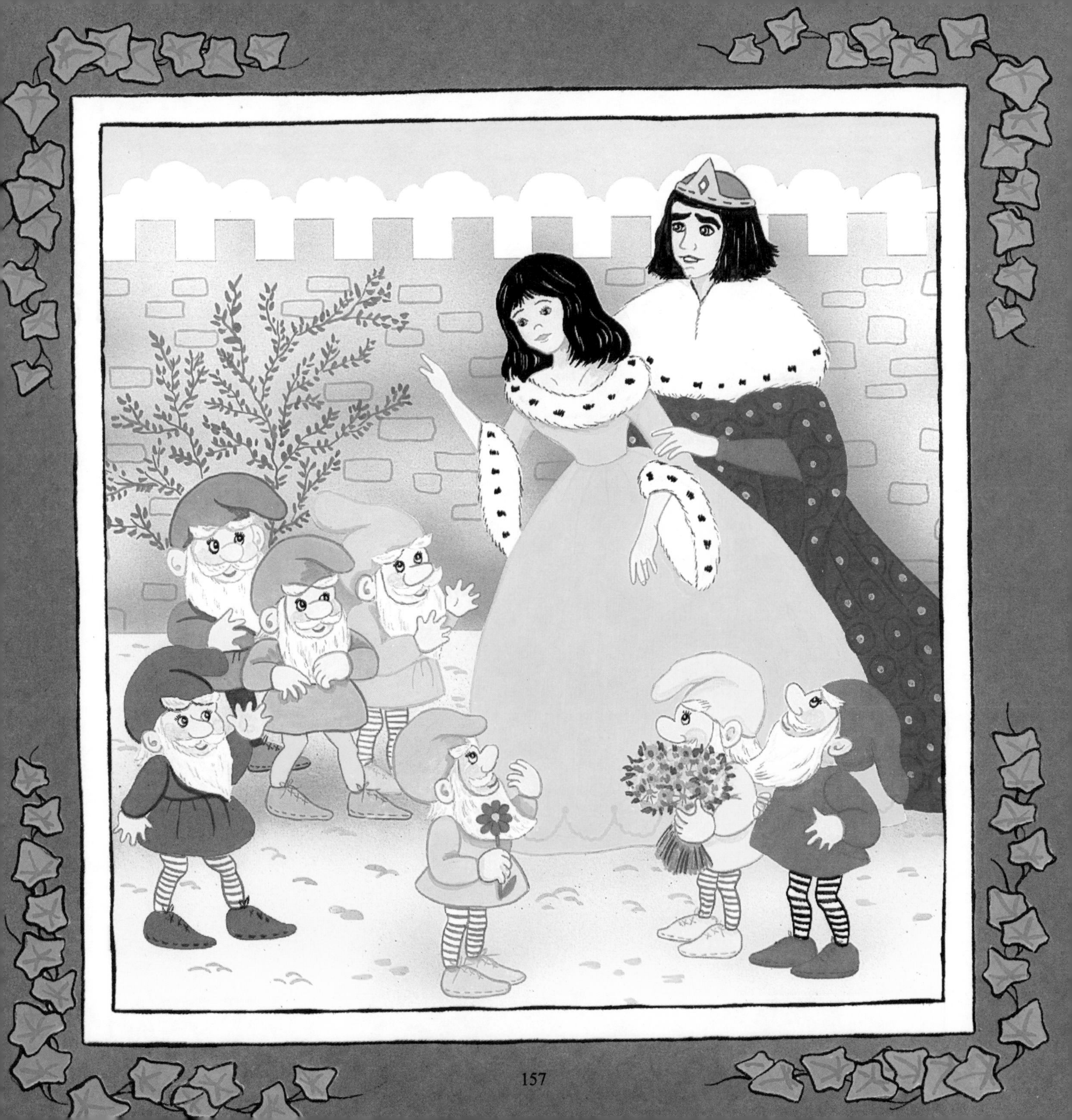

The Ugly Duckling

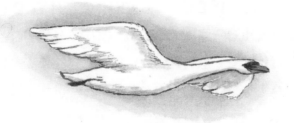

The Ugly Duckling

Once upon a time a duck sat patiently on her nest in the long grass by the river, waiting for her eggs to hatch. Suddenly the first shell cracked and out tumbled a little, yellow duckling. Then, one by one, out came the ducklings as each egg broke; that is except the biggest egg of all.

The mother duck gathered the ducklings to her and looked at the big egg, wondering why it was taking so long to hatch. Then a crack appeared in the shell and out fell the biggest and ugliest duckling you have ever seen.

"Come along, children," said the mother duck. "Come to the river and learn to swim."

So off they went to the water. Soon all the ducklings were swimming happily after their mother, but the ugly duckling was right at the back because the others laughed at him for being so big and so ugly and so different, even though he swam as well as they did.

The mother duck then took her family along to the farmyard and said,

"Now, children, this is where we will live. Stay close to me, keep away from the big cat and mind you are polite to the big rooster."

All the creatures there greeted the ducklings as they arrived but they laughed when they saw the ugly duckling and he felt very lonely and unhappy.

The poor, ugly duckling was so unhappy because everyone teased him that he ran away to the river but, even there, the creatures who saw him said,

"Goodness me, isn't he big! Isn't he ugly!"

The ugly duckling hid in the reeds and a tear dripped down his beak.

He decided to go right away and that night he set off across the fields and came to a little cottage. The old woman who lived there found him huddled on the doorstep and took him in.

Even there he was not welcome for the cat hissed at him because he could not catch mice and then hen pecked him because he could not lay eggs.

So, off he went on his travels again — across fields, over ditches and through woods — feeling more and more sad and unhappy. One day he looked up and saw some swans flying overhead.

"Oh, they are so beautiful. I wish I could be like them. I'm sure nobody laughs at them and teases them."

The poor, lonely, ugly duckling went on his way but by now summer was ending and the weather was becoming colder and food more difficult to find.

One day it was very cold and he was so tired he went to sleep while he was floating in a pond. When he awoke he could not move for the water had frozen around him while he slept.

Poor ugly duckling! He was all alone and frozen in the ice. Then he heard footsteps and saw a woodcutter coming. The duckling gave a feeble, little quack and the man went over to the pond.

"Well, what have we here? Stuck are you? Never mind, I'll soon have you free," he said and, with a few blows from his axe, he broke the ice and freed the poor, little bird. Tucking the ugly duckling under his arm he set off for home saying, "I think I'll take you home to thaw you out properly."

At his cottage he wrapped the ugly duckling up to keep him warm and told his children to look after him.

The two children were pleased to have a pet to care for and they kept the ugly duckling warm and fed him. When he had thawed out and was able to walk around again the children wanted to play with him but he was frightened and ran all around the room and knocked over the milk and eggs and the flour. The children's mother was cross when she saw all the mess and shouted,

"Outside with him! He can't stay inside here now he's better."

So, once more, the unwanted, ugly duckling ran away. He found his way to a small pond where he spent the rest of the winter, all alone and only just managing to find enough to eat.

At last the spring came, with soft breezes and warmer days, and the ugly duckling left his safe hiding place in the reeds around the pond. He spread his wings and found he could fly for, during the long, cold, dark days of winter, he had grown. He flew high above the countryside and, looking down, he saw, swimming in a lake, three of the swans he had watched when he was running away the previous year.

They looked up and called to him to join them. Hardly daring to believe that anyone wanted him he flew down. As he landed he saw his reflection in the water and cried out in joy, "I'm a swan! I'm a swan!"

Cinderella

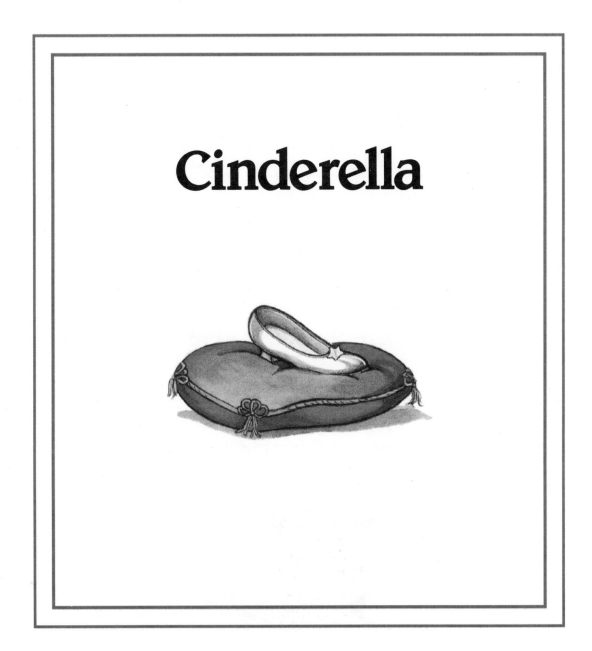

Cinderella

Once upon a time there was a young girl called Cinderella. She lived with her step-mother and two step-sisters. They were very unkind to her and ordered her about from morning until night.

"Cinderella, make the beds. Cinderella, scrub the floor."

Cinderella did all these jobs without complaining. She was a lovely girl and her ugly and bad-tempered step-sisters were very jealous of her.

Cinderella did not have a bed to sleep on; she spent the night on the hearth in the cinders. Her step-sisters had called her Cinderella because she was always covered in cinders.

One day a messenger called at the house with an invitation to a Grand Ball which the Prince was holding at the Palace.

The step-sisters' tempers were even worse than usual as they ordered Cinderella to get their fine dresses ready.

"All the handsome young men in the kingdom will be there," they cried. "We must look our best."

"Please may I come to the ball?" begged Cinderella.

"You go to the ball . . . don't be so ridiculous."

Her step-mother glared at Cinderella and said,

"You cannot go to the ball. You will have plenty of work to do once you have helped your sisters get ready."

Anyone but Cinderella would have refused to help, but she was so kind-hearted that she could not.

On the night of the ball the step-sisters had Cinderella running round in circles after them.

"Iron my dress . . . Brush my hair . . . Find my shoes."

At long last they were ready and, without a thank you or a wave goodbye, the step-sisters climbed into their carriage leaving Cinderella crying quietly all on her own next to the hearth.

"Oh, I wish I could have gone to the ball . . . I know I have nothing to wear, but I would have loved to have gone."

Suddenly, Cinderella heard a kind voice saying,

"I am your Fairy Godmother. Dry your eyes. You shall go to the ball. Just do as I ask."

Cinderella stared at the old lady who had appeared from nowhere.

"My very own Fairy Godmother. I will do as you ask," smiled Cinderella happily.

First she sent Cinderella to the garden for a pumpkin. She touched it with her magic wand and in an instant it became the most splendid coach you ever saw.

Then she asked her to bring the mousetrap from the kitchen. Inside were six white mice. The Fairy Godmother gave each a tap with her wand. Four little mice turned into magnificent white horses and the other two were changed into two fine footmen.

"Well now, Cinderella, you can go to the ball after all."

"But how can I go in these old rags?" cried Cinderella.

At once her Fairy Godmother waved her magic wand and transformed the rags into a beautiful gown, fit for a princess, and the daintiest glass slippers appeared on her feet.

"Now, off you go and enjoy yourself," said her Fairy Godmother. "But remember, you must not stay a second after midnight or all your fine clothes will turn back into rags."

"I promise I will not," said Cinderella as she set off for the ball.

When Cinderella arrived at the Palace a murmur ran around the crowd.

"Who is that beautiful girl?"

The Prince could not take his eyes off her and insisted on dancing with her for the whole evening.

Cinderella was so happy that she forgot all about the time until she heard the clock begin to strike twelve.

"Goodbye, Your Highness. I must go."

With these words, she fled from the ballroom.

In her haste Cinderella did not notice a glass slipper fall from her foot.

The Prince ran after her but she had vanished. Only the glass slipper remained.

"I will find her and make her my bride," vowed the Prince.

He sent out messengers with the glass slipper which they were to try on every girl

in the land. They finally came to Cinderella's house. The step-sisters tried it on but it would not fit.

"Why don't you try it on?" the messenger asked Cinderella.

"It won't fit," cried one step-sister. "Anyway, she wasn't at the ball."

The glass slipper fitted.

Her Fairy Godmother appeared and tapped Cinderella with her magic wand. Once more her clothes were beautiful and the messengers took her to the Palace. The Prince was overjoyed to see Cinderella.

Soon the couple were married. Everyone went to the wedding including her step-sisters whom Cinderella had completely forgiven for their previous unkindness.

Beauty &
The Beast

Beauty & The Beast

Once upon a time there lived a rich merchant who had three daughters. The elder two were rather lazy but the youngest was kind and hardworking. She was called Beauty and she loved her father very much.

Now it happened that the merchant's business ran into great difficulties and he lost all his money. The family, therefore, was forced to leave their big, fine house and move into a little cottage in the country.

The two older sisters complained endlessly that they no longer had servants to look after them but Beauty was sad for her father and did everything she could to help him. She kept the house clean and tidy and cooked the meals. She tended the garden and grew vegetables so that they always had food to eat. The merchant was worried by bills which he could not pay but still the two elder daughters grumbled about not having enough money to buy pretty dresses and jewellery.

One day the merchant was offered work in a distant town.

He instructed his daughters to look after each other while he was away and promised that he would bring each of them a present on his return.

"Bring us some shoes and pretty dresses," begged the two older sisters.

"What would you like, Beauty?" asked her father. "Just come back safely and, if you can, please bring me a bunch of white roses," replied Beauty.

All too soon it was time for the merchant to set off on his journey. Beauty stood waving at the cottage door as he rode off on his horse. It was mid-winter and the snow lay thickly on the ground. The poor horse made slow progress as it struggled through the drifts. The merchant was worried because he had hoped to reach his destination before nightfall.

Darkness began to fall as he was passing through a deep forest. In the gloom he strayed from the path and lost his way. He jumped off his horse and led it through the trees, hoping that he would find a way out of the forest. He longed for somewhere warm to rest a while. Then, just as he was giving up hope of ever seeing his three daughters again, the merchant saw, through the swirling snow, the lights of a great castle.

Thankfully, he led his horse in the direction of the lights. As he approached the door of the castle he called out but there was no answer. The lights from the castle windows shone on the stable yard and the merchant decided to stable his horse before, once again, approaching the castle door. As before, he called out when he reached the door but still there was no answer so the merchant decided to enter the castle and trust that the owner would take pity on him.

"Hello, is there anyone there?" he called as he stepped over the threshold, but he heard only the echo of his own voice. He wandered along the corridor until he found another door. On opening this he was met by a splendid sight. There was a roaring fire in the grate and in the middle of the room was a large table with a wonderful meal laid out. The merchant was so hungry that he sat at the table and ate his fill but, although he saw no-one, he had the feeling that he was being watched. At last, tired out from his journey, he slept. When he woke up the next morning, the merchant wondered where he was. Then he remembered his dreadful journey and how he had been lost in the snowstorm. He was surprised to find a new suit of clothes laid out for him and more food on the table. He ate a good breakfast and changed into the new clothes. He then went in search of the owner of the castle who had been so kind to him.

Having found no-one about, he set off for the stables to collect his horse ready to continue his journey.

He walked through a walled garden and, as it was mid-winter, he was most surprised to see that all the flowers were in full bloom and not a leaf had fallen. The merchant remembered Beauty's request for a bunch of white roses but, as he began picking them, he heard a terrible roar. Startled, he turned round quickly and saw a monstrous beast.

"Have I not given you enough that you must steal the flowers from my garden?" roared the beast. "I have fed you, clothed you and let you rest in my home and this is how you repay me. I have a good mind to punish you right now."

The merchant fell down on his knees and begged for mercy.

"I only wanted some flowers for my daughter, Beauty," he cried.

"I will let you go free," said the beast, "if one of your daughters will offer to come and live with me here. Go now and let them choose. Do not try to cheat me or I will come in search of you."

The poor merchant was so terrified that he agreed and returned to his daughters with a heavy heart. He told them the story of the castle and the terrible beast. The two older daughters refused to go and live in the castle but Beauty could not bear to see her father so unhappy. "Don't worry," she said softly. "I will go and live with the beast. I am sure no harm will come to me." So the following day the merchant and Beauty returned to the strange castle. The beast was so pleased that he gave Beauty fine dresses to wear and to the merchant he gave a chest of gold. However, he told the merchant he must leave the castle and never return. Sadly, Beauty kissed her father goodbye.

Beauty's life at the castle was very easy. Each evening the beast would come and sit with her and play beautiful music or talk and, as time passed, they became good friends.

"Are you happy, Beauty?" asked the beast one evening. "Yes, I am," replied Beauty. "There is one thing, though. I would love to see my father again."

"Then you shall visit him for a few days," replied the beast. "But you must promise to return to me within two weeks or I shall die." Beauty agreed and the next morning she left the castle. She was so happy to be home that the weeks passed by and she forgot her promise to the beast. One night, however, she had a terrible dream in which she saw the beast dying in the castle gardens. When Beauty awoke the next morning she remembered her dream and was horrified. She rushed to her horse and rode like the wind to the castle.

There she found the beast lying in the garden just as in her dream. She dropped down on her knees beside him, covered her face with her hands and began to sob. "Oh, dear Beast, I am so sorry," cried Beauty. "I will never leave you again. I love you and now I am afraid I have killed you." Her tears fell on to the beast's rough fur and slowly he began to revive. Then there was a blaze of light, the beast disappeared and in his place stood a handsome prince.

"Where is my beast?" asked a startled Beauty when she finally looked up. The prince explained that a spell had been put on him and now Beauty had broken it by loving him in spite of his ugliness.

Soon afterwards the prince and Beauty were married and her father and sisters came to the celebrations. The prince arranged for them all to stay at the castle and they lived happily ever after.

Hansel and Gretel

Hansel and Gretel

Once upon a time on the edge of a large forest there lived a poor woodcutter with his wife and their two children, Hansel and Gretel.

One night, with hardly any food left in the house, the children were sent to bed with only a piece of bread to eat. This made the woodcutter very sad and he did not know what to do.

"The only thing we can do is leave them in the forest to fend for themselves," said his wife.

He was unhappy about this but agreed. Hansel overheard this and crept silently downstairs and put two crusts of bread in his pocket.

The next morning, with Gretel leading the way, they walked into the forest. Hansel walked behind leaving a trail of breadcrumbs.

At last they were deep in the forest and the woodcutter told them to have a rest while he worked and he would come back for them later. The sound of his axe soon lulled them to sleep.

However, when they awoke they were alone and the moon was shining. Gretel began to cry.

"Don't worry, little sister, I'll soon have you home," said Hansel bravely.

Poor Hansel; when he looked for the trail of crumbs he found the forest birds had eaten every one.

"I'm sure I can remember the way home," he said and, taking hold of Gretel's hand, he led her along a path.

Alas, they were soon hopelessly lost and felt very hungry.

Suddenly, in a clearing, they saw the most extraordinary cottage. It was made of sweets and chocolate and marzipan and marshmallows.

They were so hungry that they ran up to the cottage and started to eat. The door opened and a little, old woman came out.

"Oh! You poor children. Hungry are you? Come inside and let me give you a proper meal."

When they had eaten, the old woman told them to lie down and rest.

In truth, the old woman was a wicked witch who ate little children and the very next morning, before Hansel was properly awake, she locked him in a cage. Then she made Gretel do all the work around the cottage and told her to give Hansel the tastiest morsels to eat.

"When he is good and fat I shall eat him," she chuckled wickedly.

Now the witch had very poor eyesight and each morning, when she asked Hansel to stick his finger out so she could feel if he was getting fatter, he would stick out a chicken bone instead.

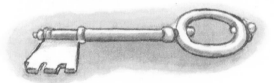

The witch could not understand why Hansel never became any fatter. In the end, she became tired of waiting and decided to eat Hansel as he was.

She ordered Gretel to make a big fire under the oven. The oven became red-hot but, because she was so short-sighted, the witch had to bend down and look closely into it to check the heat. As she did so, Gretel, as quick as a flash, pushed her inside and shut the door.

Then, joyfully, she let Hansel out of the cage.

"Now we must search the house," said Hansel. "I'm sure the witch must have treasure hidden somewhere!"

The children searched carefully and, sure enough, they found a huge chest full of coins and many jewels. In great delight they filled their pockets and Gretel also put as many as she could carry in her apron. Then they decided to find their way home through the forest.

They wandered for a long time and eventually came to a path they thought they knew. They began to run down it and there, on the edge of the forest, they could see their own cottage.

Their shouts of joy soon brought their parents out and when they saw Hansel and Gretel they hurried towards them.

As their parents greeted Hansel and Gretel they burst into tears and told them how sorry they were they had had to leave them in the forest and how much they had missed them.

The woodcutter and his wife were overjoyed to have their two children back with them and, as they picked them up and hugged them both, all the coins and jewels fell out of Gretel's apron. When the woodcutter saw them he realised that the family would never be poor again.

Their troubles were over. From then on they never went hungry again and they all lived happily ever after.

Tom Thumb

Tom Thumb

Tom Thumb was a tiny, little boy. When he was born he was hardly bigger than your thumb and that is how he got his name.

He had lived happily with his parents and six brothers until one day, when his father said,

"There is no money to buy any more food."

The boys' mother began to sob.

"My poor children! They are such good little boys."

"I am sorry, my dear, but the time has come to send our boys out into the world to seek their fortunes," he said.

"Tomorrow we'll explain the situation to the children. They are getting older now and we cannot feed so many mouths. Perhaps they will find their fortunes."

When the boys were told the next morning, they set off excitedly there and then. The whole day proved to be an adventure but, when night came, they wanted to return home.

Even though Tom Thumb was the smallest of the brothers, he was the cleverest. He had carefully dropped pebbles as they had walked during the day and was now able to lead his brothers home.

Once they were safely inside they talked excitedly about their adventures and were quite happy to set off again the next morning. Their mother had spent the evening making up seven little bundles for them. She put a change of clothes and a piece of bread in each bundle.

Their parents had decided to walk part of the way with them before saying goodbye. The boys walked on a long way on their own but still they did not come to the town where they had hoped to offer their services to anyone who would employ them.

At last they saw a house and decided to ask for shelter for the night. They did not know that the house belonged to an ogre who ate children.

Tom Thumb was sent to knock on the door and when the ogre's wife opened it she was at first scared to let them in. But then, feeling sorry for the boys, she said they could stay but would have to hide when the ogre returned home.

As soon as they heard the ogre's footsteps they quickly hid under a cupboard. Tom Thumb hid behind a basket of wood.

Suddenly the ogre began to sniff loudly round the kitchen.

"Fee, fi, fo, fum. I smell the blood of a little one. It can't be the girls I am going to eat tomorrow as they are safely tucked up in bed and I have locked the door."

Then he saw the brothers and grinned.

"Aha! What a feast I am going to have tomorrow!" he cried, as he grabbed them in his huge arms and locked them in the room with the seven little girls.

The boys were frightened and exhausted and fell asleep.

Tom Thumb had, in the meantime, crept out of his hiding place and, finding the key to the door, had woken his brothers and the little girls and they were just about to escape when the ogre came thundering in.

They made a dash for the door, slipped between the ogre's legs and out through the front door they fled. The ogre ran after them but the children were too quick for him. He lay panting on the ground while they made their escape. The little girls told the seven brothers where they lived and together they went to find the girls' mother.

Their mother was so happy when she saw the children. When Tom Thumb told her what had happened not only did she want to give Tom a reward but she wanted to take Tom and his brothers back to their parents in the woods. She gave them a bag of gold coins, telling them to give them to their parents so that they would never want for anything for the rest of their days.

Their parents were so happy to see the boys again. They had wanted to save the children from starvation but they had had a terrible time worrying about them. But now, with the bag of gold coins, they would all be able to live together again, as happy as they had been before.

The Pied Piper of Hamelin

The Pied Piper of Hamelin

There is a town in Germany called Hamelin and, a long time ago, disaster struck. Thousands and thousands of rats appeared as if out of nowhere. They were not just ordinary rats; they were big, bold rats and could not be frightened away.

They were in the houses, eating all the food they could find. They were in the schools, nipping the children and destroying their books.

When the food supplies started running out, the rats began to eat the furniture. They climbed over the beds, hung on to the curtains and could be seen scampering over the roof-tops. The people of Hamelin tried everything to rid themselves of the rats.

Every day there seemed to be twice as many rats as the day before. Soon there was very little food or drink left for the towns-people and they were desperate to get rid of the rats.

Mothers tried their best to protect their babies in their cradles from the ugly rats but it was not easy. Everyone was very angry as they thought that the Mayor and the Town Council did not seem to be doing anything to solve the problem so they called a meeting in the town square. When all the townspeople had gathered, they marched to the Town Hall. There they demanded of the Mayor and his Councillors that they do something to end the plague of rats. The angry crowd frightened the Mayor and the Town Council into action.

"There must be someone who can rid us of these rats," said one of the Councillors. "Why don't we offer a reward to anyone who can help us?"

Now the Mayor, who was very greedy and loath to part with money unless it was spent on himself, was not too happy with this suggestion. At last he had to agree because he could not think of any other solution himself.

The next day the town crier was sent out through the streets to announce the decision taken by the Mayor and reward posters were pinned on every available wall and tree both in Hamelin itself and the surrounding district.

THERE WILL BE A REWARD OF

1,000 GUILDERS

GIVEN TO THE PERSON WHO RIDS

THE TOWN OF HAMELIN OF RATS.

People came from far and wide and tried all sorts of methods to rid the town of its rat problem but all failed. No matter what they did, it seemed as if the rats were there to stay. Then one day, when the townspeople had almost given up hope, a stranger walked into town. He made his way to the Town Hall and asked to speak to the Mayor and his Council.

The townspeople had followed the stranger to the Town Hall as they were intrigued by his clothes and his manner, for he was quite unlike anyone they had ever seen before. The colours he wore were bright and bold, his cape reached down to the floor and in his pointed hat was a long, peacock feather. Tucked into his belt was a long, thin pipe.

The Mayor, seated in his parlour, was quite startled when the stranger arrived. "Who are you?" he asked. "People call me the Pied Piper," answered the stranger. "I have seen your notice offering a reward for ridding your town of rats so I have come to do just that and claim the reward." The Mayor thought it highly unlikely that this strange-looking man would be able to do this but he said, "If there are no rats left in Hamelin by dawn, you shall have the reward."

"Just how do you plan on doing this?" asked a member of the Council.

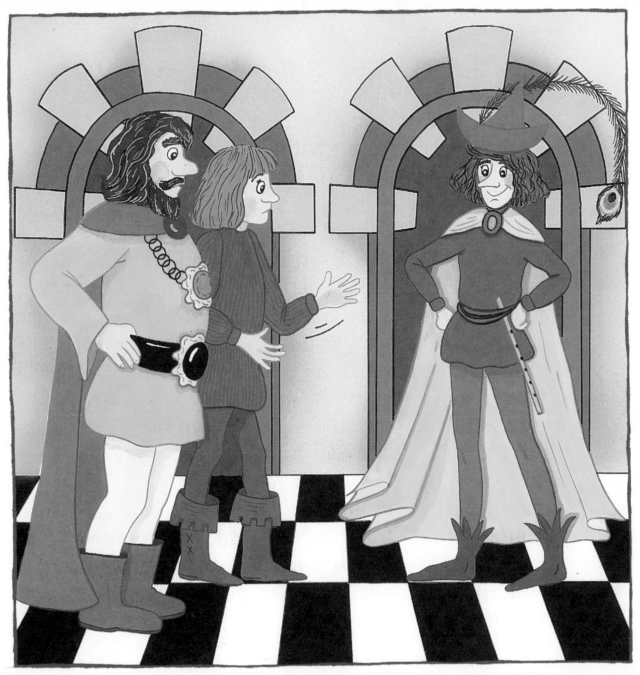

"By means of my magic pipe I can rid Hamelin of its rats. No creature on earth can resist its music," replied the Pied Piper.

"Well, get on with it then," said the impatient Mayor. "Go. Play your music and work your magic."

The Pied Piper stepped out into the street, took the pipe from his belt and put it to his lips. He began to play a weird, mournful melody which was quite unlike any music ever heard before. Suddenly, rats appeared from everywhere, out of every nook and cranny, every doorway and every alleyway. The Pied Piper started walking down the street and the rats followed him. On and on he walked, through the town square, past the school where the children were staring open-mouthed at the stranger. The Pied Piper played on making his way through all the streets of Hamelin followed by thousands and thousands of rats.

The rats were all shapes and sizes and were mesmerized by the tune played by the stranger. They were tripping over each other in their haste to follow the Pied Piper.

He continued to walk right across the town to the water's edge. There he stepped into a boat and floated down the river, all the while continuing to play his haunting music. The rats, still following the music, plunged into the river.

All night the Pied Piper's music could be heard, accompanied by the squealing of the rats as they drowned. At sunrise, all was quiet. Every last rat had been drowned.

The Mayor was so happy the rats had gone that he arranged a huge banquet for the townspeople. They all gathered in the town square, singing and dancing. It was such a relief for them not to see or hear those horrible rats. Then the Pied Piper went to collect his reward from the Mayor.

The Mayor was not pleased to see the Pied Piper and actually refused to pay him his reward.

"You promised me one thousand guilders," said the Pied Piper. "You said you would give a reward to anyone who got rid of the rats. Well, I have got rid of them for you."

"Oh, come now, my good man," said the Mayor. "All you did was play a tune on that pipe of yours. That wasn't very difficult and doesn't deserve a reward."

"You will be sorry," replied the Pied Piper. "I can play other tunes, you know."

"Go away and play your pipe," said the Mayor. "You don't frighten me."

At this, the Pied Piper turned and walked out of the Town Hall. When he was in the town square he put his pipe to his lips and played the sweetest music you have ever heard. It was music which no child could resist and the children loved it.

They came out from their homes laughing and chattering, not knowing where the Pied Piper and his music would lead them, but happy and eager to follow him. Their mothers called after them but they did not take any notice. It was as if they could hear only the music.

On and on they walked, past the river and through the fields, making their way steadily to the mountains. Unbelievably, as they reached the highest mountain it opened up and the Pied Piper and the children walked in. The mountain closed after them and they were never seen again.

Without the children Hamelin was a quiet, unhappy town. The mothers and fathers were so angry with the Mayor that they chased him and his Councillors out of the town. It was many, many years before the sound of children's laughter could be heard in the playgrounds and streets of Hamelin.

The Little Mermaid

The Little Mermaid

Once upon a time there was a little mermaid, the youngest, and most beautiful, daughter of the Mer King. She lived with her father, grandmother and five sisters in a palace of shells, deep, deep in the ocean. The mermaids longed to see the world above that their grandmother had described but each had to wait until her fifteenth birthday.

At last her birthday came and the little mermaid rose to the surface and gazed about in wonder.

A large galleon was nearby and she could hear music. A Prince was celebrating his birthday and she thought he was the most handsome being she had ever seen.

Suddenly a storm blew up. The waves grew higher until at last they overwhelmed the proud ship. She was horrified to see the Prince sinking, apparently lifeless. She swam quickly to him and pulled him to the surface.

When the storm passed she took him to land and laid him on a beach and then shyly hid to see what would happen.

Some girls found the Prince and he was taken to their castle and the little mermaid swam back to her father's palace thinking sadly that the Prince would never know it was she who had saved him and that she would never see him again.

One of her sisters knew the palace where the Prince lived so the little mermaid spent hours watching him for she had fallen deeply in love.

Her grandmother explained that mer-people live for three hundred years but when they die they become sea-foam, as they have no souls. She said that humans, although they only live for a short time, have souls and so, when they die, go to a wonderful place far away.

"Is there any way I can get a soul?" asked the little mermaid.

"Only if a human falls in love with you and that is unlikely for humans like legs not tails."

In desperation she sought help from the Sea Witch. It was a terrifying, dangerous journey but the thought of the Prince gave her courage.

"So you want legs? Foolish child! Losing your tail is painful and walking on feet will be like walking on knives. If he loves another you will become sea-foam."

"Please, I still want to try."

"I must have your voice in payment for this potion," growled the Witch and, so in love was the little mermaid, she agreed.

She swam to the Prince's palace before she drank the potion. She felt a sharp pain, fell into a deep sleep and awoke with human legs.

The Prince asked who the lovely stranger was but she could only smile. He grew fond of the girl with the sweet smile who danced so elegantly (even though it was as if she danced on knives) but he did not ask her to marry him and one day he told her he was to marry a foreign princess.

"I am sure I can love only the girl I glimpsed when she saved me from drowning. You look a little like her and if I must marry someone else I would rather marry you."

Her eyes filled with tears for she could not speak to tell him the truth.

The little mermaid travelled with the Prince to his wedding and he was glad when he found his bride was one of the girls who had found him on the beach because he thought she was his rescuer and fell in love with her.

At the feast on the Prince's ship after the wedding the little mermaid thought her heart would break.

She wept, for at dawn she would die and become sea-foam. As she stood there her sisters came, pale and with all their long hair gone.

"We gave our hair to the Sea Witch as payment for a magic knife. If you kill the Prince with it before dawn you will be a mermaid again," they cried.

They gave her the knife and she went to where the Prince was asleep but, even to save herself, she could not kill him and, with one last loving look, she threw herself into the sea and became sea-foam.

As the sun rose higher she found herself high in the sky.

"Where am I?" she asked and the reply came from sweet voices in the glowing lights around her.

"You are with the Children of the Air. We earn our souls by helping those who suffer and you can earn a soul too."

Below the Prince and his bride sailed on not knowing the little mermaid was smiling down at them.

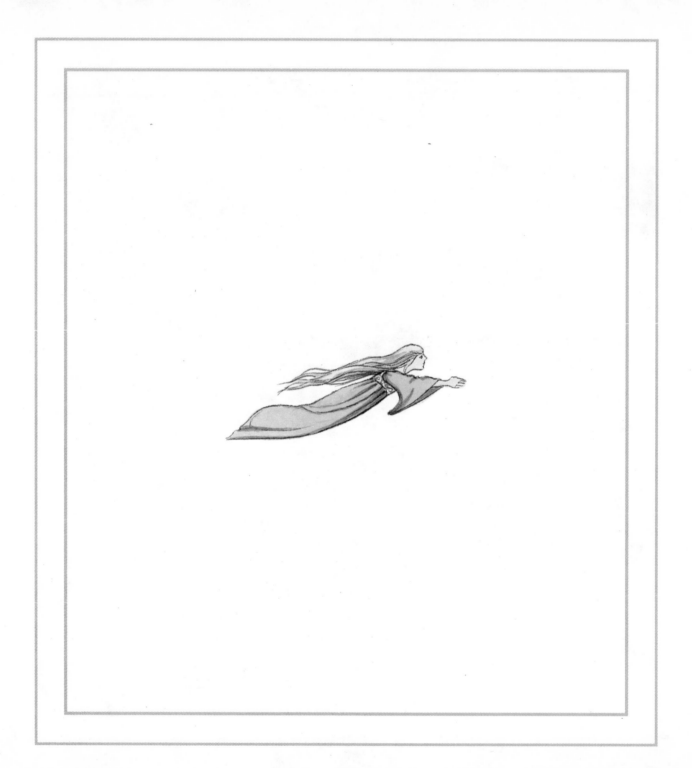

Little Red Riding Hood

Little Red Riding Hood

Once upon a time there was a little girl who was known to all as Little Red Riding Hood, as she never went out without her red cape with its red hood.

One morning, Little Red Riding Hood's mother baked a cake and said to Little Red Riding Hood, "I want you to take this cake to your grandmother, please. She is not well and I am sure it will cheer her up. Remember to keep to the path and do not take the short cut through the wood."

So Little Red Riding Hood set off for her grandmother's house but, when she came to the wood, she forgot her mother's warning and took the short cut. As she was walking along she met a wolf. He fell into step beside her and asked, "What have you got in your basket, little girl?"

"It is a cake for my grandmother," replied Little Red Riding Hood.

The wolf was forming a plan.

"What is your name?" he asked. "And where does your grandmother live?"

"My name is Little Red Riding Hood," she replied. "And my grandmother lives in the little cottage near the bridge."

Then Little Red Riding Hood saw some pretty flowers and stopped to pick a bunch for her grandmother so the wolf said goodbye and raced off. He took the shortest way through the wood to Grandmother's cottage. He was already thinking about his next meal as he knocked on the cottage door. "Who's there?" called Grandmother. "It's Little Red Riding Hood," said the wolf in a small, squeaky voice. "I've brought you a cake and some flowers." Grandmother was in bed and not very well so she called, "Pull up the latch and come in, my dear."

As soon as Grandmother saw the wolf she jumped out of bed and locked herself in a cupboard.

Then the wolf put on Grandmother's shawl and cap and jumped into bed to wait for Little Red Riding Hood. He did not have long to wait before she knocked on the door. "Who's there?" he called, doing his best to make his voice sound like Grandmother's. "It's Little Red Riding Hood with a cake from Mother and some flowers," came the reply. "Come in, dear," called the wolf. Little Red Riding Hood thought Grandmother sounded rather strange but she opened the door and stepped inside. "Grandmother, how strange you look today," said Little Red Riding Hood. "What big eyes you have!"

"All the better to see you with, my dear," replied the wolf.

"And what big teeth you have," cried the little girl.

"All the better to eat you with," growled the wolf. And, saying this, he leapt out of bed to grab Little Red Riding Hood.

"Help!" she screamed. "Save me!" At that moment the door was thrown open and in rushed a woodcutter. He had been chopping logs nearby when he heard Little Red Riding Hood's screams. When the wolf saw the woodcutter with his great, big axe he jumped through the open window and ran as fast as he could, but he tripped and fell headlong into a well and was never seen again.

Meanwhile, Grandmother came out of the cupboard and gave Little Red Riding Hood a great, big hug. "Oh, Grandmother, I was so frightened," said Little Red Riding Hood. "So was I," replied Grandmother, "but we are safe now." They thanked the woodcutter for saving them and invited him to stay for tea. When they had eaten, Grandmother went back to bed and, as it was growing dark, the woodcutter lifted Little Red Riding Hood on to his shoulders and carried her home. How surprised her mother was to hear the story!